Thoughtful Thinking

Poems for Children

Daksha Patel

Grosvenor House
Publishing Limited

This book is published by
Grosvenor House Publishing Ltd
Link House
140 The Broadway, Tolworth, Surrey, KT6 7HT.
www.grosvenorhousepublishing.co.uk

A CIP record for this book
is available from the British Library

ISBN 978-1-80381-130-7
eBook ISBN 978-1-80381-258-8

Dedication

I dedicate this book to my family and Swami Vivekananda,

who is my role model.

CONTENTS

ABOUT THE AUTHOR

Daksha Patel is of Indian origin, born in October 1975. Daksha has a BA Honours Degree in English with History, and a Post Graduate Certificate in Primary Education, including the Qualified Teacher Status, from Brunel University. She is also fluent in Gujarati and holds a purple belt in Karate.

Daksha's previous publications include *Thoughtful Thinking - Short Stories for Children*, published by GHP and *Natural Knowledge Comprehension Book,* published by Olympia Publishers.

Daksha's motto in life is: "if at first you don't succeed in your aims and objectives then you should try, try and try again"; as she believes that education is for character-building and enables us to shine like stars when we succeed.

THE FALCON

The thunderous claws, keen to touch,
The ecstatic body of a moving machine,
Feathers of pride, puffed to heights,
Scanning like a radar.
The sudden wait...
Before a wondrous beauty takes flight,
A feast for elegant claws meets the sights,
While wings are pounding,
Beating the air.
A moving shadow casts,
Before a sunset,
He dominates earth and air.
The red sky is pierced with a bullet.

By Ms Daksha Patel

The Falcon Poem Comprehension

1) What is a falcon a type of?

2) Can a falcon fly?

3) What features does a falcon have?

4) How do a falcon's features help it to hunt?

5) Are there words in the poem that rhyme?

6) Which words in the poem rhyme?

7) Is the falcon beautiful?

8) Find the alliteration in the poem.

9) Is the falcon's body compared to a machine?

10) What is meant by 'He dominates earth and air'?

Falcon Poem Comprehension Answers

1. A bird.

2. Yes.

3. Claws, eyes, beak.

4. The claws rip apart flesh.
   The wings help the bird to fly.
   The eyes help the bird to find its prey on the ground.

5. Yes.

6. Flight and sight.

7. Yes.

8. Moving machine. Pride Puffed.

9. Yes.

10. He rules earth and air because of his ability to hunt on ground and in the air.

COBRA

I have no arms,
I have no legs,
I smell with my tongue.
If someone harms me,
I hiss,
I raise my hood,
And inject,
My deadly venom.

By Ms Daksha Patel

Cobra Poem Comprehension

1) What is a cobra?

2) What is the onomatopoeic word in the poem?

3) What countries can you find cobras in?

4) Is a cobra dangerous?

5) Are there different types of cobras?

6) Why does the cobra 'hiss' in the poem?

7) What happens when the cobra injects its venom?

8) Do people die from snake bites?

9) The cobra is a type of reptile. What does that mean?

10) How does the cobra smell things?

Cobra Poem Comprehension Answers

1. A snake.

2. Hiss.

3. India, China, Indonesia, Philippines, Burma, Sri Lanka, Bangladesh and Africa.

4. Yes.

5. Yes.

6. To warn you before it strikes.

7. You get poisoned.

8. Yes.

9. It is cold-blooded.

10. With its tongue.

DECEMBER TIME

Winter is here,
Christmas is coming,
Snow is falling,
And children are singing.

The aromas of food and wine
Linger in Christian homes.
While trees are bare outside,
But inside there is mistletoe.

Winter is here,
Christmas is coming,
Snow is falling,
And children are singing.

The Christmas trees shine through peoples windows,
As houses are covered with lights and tinsel.

Winter is here,
Christmas is coming,
Snow is falling,
And children are singing.

The snow is like a blanket on the ground,
With snow balls the people are fighting.

Winter is here,
Christmas is coming,
Snow is falling,
And children are singing.

By Ms Daksha Patel

December Time Poem Comprehension

1) What is this poem about?

2) What season is this poem dealing with?

3) Is it a 'White Christmas' in the poem?

4) Why are children 'singing'?

5) What is 'mistletoe' for?

6) What are people decorating their houses with?

7) When the poem says that 'people are fighting' is it a good thing or bad thing?

8) Have you ever played with 'Snow'?

9) Which part of the poem do you like?

10) Does the poem remind you of your Christmases?

December Time Poem
Comprehension Answers

1. Christmas.

2. Winter.

3. Yes.

4. Because it is Christmas.

5. You kiss someone under the mistletoe.

6. A Christmas tree, lights and tinsel.

7. A good thing.

8. Yes or No.

9. Your own opinion.

10. Yes or No.

HAIKU:
BEEHIVE

Sweet scent of honey
Roaming the fresh morning air.
The bees hard at work.

By Ms Daksha Patel

Haiku: Beehive Poem Comprehension

1) What is a 'Haiku'?

2) What is a beehive?

3) Is the smell of honey 'Sweet'?

4) Is honey sweet to taste?

5) Why are the bees 'hard at work'?

6) Who makes the honey in the beehive?

7) Are bees useful?

8) Where in the poem is alliteration used?

9) Can bees harm us?

10) Have you ever been stung by a bee?

The Beehive Poem Comprehension Answers

1. Japanese Poetry.

2. A place to house bees in.

3. Yes.

4. Yes.

5. They are making honey.

6. The bees.

7. Yes.

8. Sweet scent in the first line.

9. Yes.

10. Yes or No.

MORNING

Blue is the sky.
White is the light.
The sun rays shine
Ever so bright.
From the roof tops of houses in Devon
There lies heaven.

By Ms Daksha Patel

Morning Poem Comprehension

1) What is this poem about?

2) What colour is the sky?

3) What rhymes in the poem?

4) What rhymes with 'Devon'?

5) What words make the poem descriptive?

6) What does 'Heaven' mean to you?

7) Do you have a special place that you like?

8) Have you ever been on 'a roof top'?

9) What is the weather like in the poem?

10) Have you ever been to 'Devon'?

Morning Poem Comprehension Answers

1. Devon.

2. Blue.

3. Light and bright. Heaven and Devon.

4. Heaven.

5. The adjectives in the poem.

6. An ideal place to live in.

7. Your opinion.

8. Yes or No.

9. Sunny.

10. Yes or No.

RAINBOW POEM

R is the Red hot lava from a volcano.

O is the Orange colour of a satsuma.

Y is for the Yellow when the sun is seen at a distance.

G is the Green grass that grows beneath our feet.

B is the Blue sky without clouds.

I is for the Indigo-coloured waters of the Caribbean.

V is for the Violet flowers that grow on islands.

By Ms Daksha Patel

Rainbow Poem Comprehension

1) What is a 'Rainbow'?

2) Have you ever seen a rainbow?

3) What conditions do you need to get a rainbow showing?

4) Can there be rain and sunshine at the same time?

5) What are the colours of the rainbow?

6) Can you find the rainbow colours in the poem?

7) What is a 'volcano'?

8) What is a 'satsuma'?

9) What colour is 'Indigo'?

10) What colour is 'Violet'?

Rainbow Poem Comprehension Answers

1. A curved band of colours seen in the sky when the sun shines through rain.

2. Yes or No.

3. Sun and rain at the same time.

4. Yes.

5. Red, Orange, Yellow, Green, Blue, Indigo, and Violet.

6. Yes.

7. A mountain with an opening at the top from which lava etc and hot gases flow.

8. A fruit.

9. A blue colour.

10. A purple colour.

THE SWAN

With pure, pearly, white feathers,
The swan is a symbol of purity,
Of love and fidelity,
A mate for life.
This birdy can lay up to eight eggs.

With waterproof feathers,
And a streamline body,
This bird floats, dives, glides and swims in water.
It looks like a white jet-ski on the water.

When searching for food,
Blessed is the swan with its
Webbed feet,
Long neck,
And strong beak,
For swans eat mostly vegetation.

Swans, they migrate to different places.
They have large powerful wings
To fly far.

On the regal and graceful white swan,
Sits Saraswati (the Goddess of Wisdom).
She rides the swan of royal and good qualities.
The swan's natural gift is:
To separate milk from water with its beak.
This appeals to the Hindu Deity too,
For Saraswati, tells us to discriminate
between good and bad
And take only the good.

By Ms Daksha Patel

The Swan Poem Comprehension

1) What type of animal is a swan?

2) Where is there alliteration in the poem?

3) What is the swan compared to in water?

4) Why is the swan 'Blessed'?

5) Who is 'Saraswati'?

6) What is the swan's 'natural gift'?

7) What does it mean to 'discriminate' in the context of this poem?

8) What is a 'streamline body'?

9) Are all swans 'white'?

10) Why are swans a symbol of 'love'?

The Swan Poem Comprehension Answers

1. A bird.

2. Pure, pearly.

3. A white jet-ski.

4. The swan is blessed because of its fully functioning body, beauty, and features which help the swan to find food and feed to stay alive. Also, the swan is useful for designing things like filters and the white jet-ski.

5. The Hindu Goddess of Wisdom.

6. To separate milk from water with its beak.

7. To make an informed choice between good and bad.

8. A body that works well in water. The swan floats, dives, glides, and swims in water.

9. No.

10. They stay together for life.

ME

In the morning, brushing my teeth white,
I clear the plaque.
I wash my face and body clean.
I dress the Hindu Deity.
I ring a bell,
I light the diva and incense sticks.
I burn the camphor, and sprinkle water.
Then, I look in the mirror and see a reflection of me.

Me, me, not you.

In the afternoon, at school I read and write.
Scribbling on paper until its right.
I do my sums and sit for exams and tests.
I study all I can for

Me, me, not you.

At lunchtime, I eat.
I chew, chew, chew the food in my mouth.
I eat for

Me, me, not you.

Then, in the evening,
I do my Puja.
I light the lamp again,
It's a yellow flame.
I watch the Television for

Me, me, not you.

At night, I sleep.
I dream of my day and me.
The bed sheets are as fluffy as snow and comfortable
for

Me, me, not you.

There is nobody I would rather be than me!
This poem is about me and my day. It's about

Me, me, not you.

By Ms Daksha Patel

Me Poem Comprehension

1) Who is this poem about?

2) What is a 'Hindu Deity'?

3) How is the day split up in the poem?

4) What effect does 'I chew, chew, chew' have in the poem?

5) What is 'Puja'?

6) Do you have a daily routine like the one in the poem?

7) Who is important in the poem?

8) Is 'Me' a selfish poem?

9) What age do you think the author is in the poem?

10) Does the author like herself?

Me Poem Comprehension Answers

1. Daksha Patel, the author of this book.

2. An image of a God or Goddess.

3. Morning, afternoon, evening and night.

4. It feels like you are eating it yourself.

5. Hindu ritual worship.

6. Yes or No.

7. Me, the author.

8. Yes or No.

9. Guess it.

10. Yes.

RED

Red is the colour that angers and provokes the bull.

It is the colour of danger and warning.

Red tells us to stop!

It is the striking colour of style to dress in red,

To stand out!

Red is a lucky colour in Indian culture.

It is an auspicious colour for an Indian bride.

Red is the colour of fire, the sari of the Goddess Laxmi.

Red is the powder (called kum kum)
used in marking the tilak on the foreheads of Hindu's.

It is the colour of the great red spot on Jupiter.

Red is the spot made from a laser pen to point out
information.

It is the colour one sees when one is angry.

Red, red, red!

By Ms Daksha Patel

Red Poem Comprehension

1) What colour provokes a bull?

2) What is the main colour of danger and warning signs?

3) Do traffic lights turn red?

4) Does red stand out?

5) Is it good to write in red if you are Hindu?

6) What colour is the great red spot on Jupiter?

7) What is 'Kum Kum'?

8) Who is Laxmi?

9) What is an exclamation mark?

10) Where are there exclamation marks in the poem 'Red'?

Red Poem Comprehension Answers

1. Red.

2. Red.

3. Yes

4. Yes.

5. Yes.

6. Red.

7. A red powder to mark on the forehead of Hindus.

8. The Goddess of wealth.

9. A punctuation mark.

10. The 3rd line of the poem, the 5th line of the poem and the end line of the poem.

HURRICANE IRMA (2017)

Hurricane Irma was ever so firmer than
Katrina ever was,
She smashed up houses and split up spouses,
Without a care in the world.

Irma created large floods,
Throwing debris including mud.

In the gusts,
She spilt some blood,
Regardless of age or creed.

Cuba, Antigua and Barbuda were some of
those who faced Irma's wrath,
Regaining strength from the seas
she was set to hit the Florida Keys.

Irma was the size of France,
The Americans evaluated this in advance,
Knowing her presence was near,
Most thought 'It's too dangerous to stay here'.

She flattened the Keys,
Leaving people crying on their knees,
But if they were in England,
Dot would be making them teas.

She left the people of Florida in tears,
Looking for their peers,
Exposed and bare,
With debris around everywhere.

Rebuilding will be hard,
But don't let down your guard,
Because hurricane Jose isn't afar.

By Ms Daksha Patel

Hurricane Irma (2017) Comprehension

1) What is this poem about?

2) What is a hurricane?

3) Which countries did 'Hurricane Irma' hit?

4) What happened to the people in the way of the hurricane?

5) What was Irma the size of?

6) Why would Dot be making tea?

7) What does Jose refer to?

8) How would you feel if you lost your property or even your loved ones in a hurricane?

9) What is the common poetic device used mostly throughout the poem?

10) Where would you go if you knew a category five hurricane was coming your way?

Hurricane Irma Poem
Comprehension Answers

1. A hurricane.

2. A bad weather condition.

3. Cuba, Antigua and Barbuda, and Florida.

4. Property and life was harmed.

5. France.

6. Dot Cotton is a character from an English soap called Eastenders. She is always making people teas to calm them down when they get problems.

7. Another hurricane.

8. Bad and in tears.

9. Rhyming.

10. To a hurricane shelter or a very strong building.

SWEET SHOP POEM

Humbugs are stripy like zebras.
Liquorice is black or red in long laces,
Cola bottles are like gummy bears and rings
-They are soft, clear and chewy.
Pick'n'Mix sweets come in all shapes, colours and sizes.

You suck the sweets down to zero.
Some are squishy and soft,
While others are hard boiled and need some teeth.

Sweets defer in texture and taste.
Soft centred sweets ooze out with edible paste.
The juices race around your mouth when you eat sweets.
Especially, sweet and sour sweets.

There are no bitter sweets,
But when you stand by the Pick'n'Mix
There is a rainbow of colours
To entice children to buy those sweets.
Sometimes people even refer to me as 'sweet.'

By Ms Daksha Patel

Sweet Shop Poem Comprehension

1) Name some types of sweets from the poem?

2) What is Pick'n'Mix?

3) Do you like eating sweets?

4) Are sweets good for your teeth?

5) Why are sweets so colourful?

6) Name some of your favourite sweets?

7) What is the meaning of calling another person 'sweet'?

8) Name the shapes of some sweets you know?

9) Why do you have to suck some sweets?

10) Are sweets just for children?

Sweet Shop Poem Comprehension Answers

1. Humbugs, Liquorice, Cola bottles, Gummy bears, Gummy rings.

2. A self-serving sweet counter.

3. Yes or No.

4. No.

5. To entice people to buy them.

6. Your own choice.

7. They are kind.

8. Oval, cube, round, flat, etc

9. To make smaller and get the flavour out.

10. No.

HAIKU:
APPLE ORCHARD

It is the ripe smell
Of apples that lingers in
The cold morning air.

By Ms Daksha Patel

Apple Orchard Poem Comprehension

1) What is an Orchard?

2) What is this poem about?

3) Identify a verb in the poem?

4) Identify an adjective that is used in the poem?

5) Identify one preposition word in the poem?

6) Do you eat apples?

7) Are all apples green?

8) Do all apples have seeds in them?

9) How do you know when an apple is rotten?

10) How many different ways is there to eat an apple?

Apple Orchard Poem
Comprehension Answers

1. An apple farm.

2. An apple Orchard.

3. Lingers, smell.

4. Cold.

5. In.

6. Yes or No.

7. No.

8. Yes.

9. It looks bad, and it smells.

10. You can eat it raw, boil it, steam it, cook it in the oven, fry it, freeze it, and juice it.

WHALE POEM

The whales are air breathing,
And warm-blooded mammals.
The fat under their skin keeps them warm.

Living in the deep blue sea,
They look like fish,
But, without scales.
They are silky smooth with no hair.

With a Torpedo-shaped body,
They swim far and fast.
The whales are suited to a marine life.
A life spent in water.

Eating the small plankton,
The whale is huge in contrast.

The whales feed and search,
For a mate to reproduce with,
So they can have a future, together.
As a family of whales,
They are happy together.
The pride of progeny is in them too.

By Ms Daksha Patel

Whale Poem Comprehension

1) Are whales mammals?

2) What keeps the whales warm in the sea?

3) Where do whales live?

4) What weapon is the whale compared to?

5) Can whales swim?

6) What do whales eat?

7) Is plankton small or big?

8) Find a metaphor in the poem.

9) Are humans mammals?

10) Where is the alliteration in the poem?

Whale Poem Comprehension Answers

1. Yes.

2. The fat under the skin.

3. In the sea.

4. A Torpedo.

5. Yes.

6. Plankton.

7. Small.

8. A Torpedo-shaped body.

9. Yes.

10. Silky smooth.

HAIKU:
PIZZA POEM

A round pizza base,
With tasty toppings on it.
Cheese stretching like lace.

By Ms Daksha Patel

Haiku: Pizza Poem Comprehension

1) Which words in the poem rhyme?

2) Find the alliterations in the poem.

3) Find the simile in the poem.

4) What shape is the pizza?

5) Do you like pizza?

6) What is the preposition word in the poem?

7) What is stretching in the poem?

8) Can you make a pizza?

9) Have you ever brought a pizza from a pizza shop?

10) Name some pizza toppings.

Pizza Poem Comprehension Answers

1. Base and lace.

2. Tasty toppings and like lace.

3. Cheese stretching like lace.

4. Round.

5. Yes or No.

6. On.

7. Cheese.

8. Yes or No.

9. Yes or No.

10. Quorn, meat, cheese, vegetables, fish, fruit and herbs.

HAIKU:
STRAWBERRY PICKING POEM

Seeds on the outside,
With red bumpy flesh to eat.
Hands picking quickly.

By Ms Daksha Patel

Strawberry Picking Poem Comprehension

1) What is this poem about?

2) Where are the seeds of the strawberries?

3) What colour are the strawberries?

4) What colour are strawberry seeds?

5) Do you eat the seeds of the strawberry?

6) What part of the body do you use to pick strawberries?

7) Who eats strawberries?

8) What is a strawberry a type of?

9) Why must the strawberries be picked quickly?

10) Have you been to a farm where strawberries are grown there?

Strawberry Picking Comprehension Answers

1. Picking strawberries.

2. On the outside of each berry.

3. Red.

4. Green or yellow.

5. Yes.

6. The hands.

7. Humans, animals, birds, insects.

8. Fruit or berry.

9. So they don't spoil.

10. Yes or No.

GLOSSARY

<u>Adjectives</u> are describing (descriptive) words such as: striped, moving, furry.

<u>Adverbs</u> tell you how it's done, such as how someone eats, e.g. quickly.

<u>Alliteration</u> is the repeating of a sound, e.g. The snake slithered slowly.

<u>Haikus</u>: short poems from Japan — they have three lines and 17 syllables in total.

<u>Metaphor</u> is when you compare something to something else without using 'like' or 'as'.

<u>Nouns</u> are naming words such as: Daksha, Africa and door.

<u>Onomatopoeia</u> is a word used to make a sound, e.g. bang, click, hiss.

<u>Personification</u> is something that has human quality that is attached to something like an object, e.g. the black board stares and the leaves smile.

<u>Prepositions</u> are where we or something is situated, e.g. We are *under* the bridge.

<u>Rhyme</u> is when the ending of the poem has the same sound as previous lines.

<u>Simile</u> is when you describe something similar to something else using the words 'like' or 'as'.

<u>Superlative</u> describes the highest degree of a quality (adjective or adverb), e.g. bravest, most beautiful.

<u>Verbs</u> are doing words such as jump, dive, sing.

<u>The difference between a verse and a stanza</u> is that verses are all equal and stanzas are chunks that are not equal.

SOURCES/BIBLIOGRAPHY

Books Seen and Read:

- The Illustrated Encyclopedia of Wildlife, Volume 1, Pages 10-11.
- First Poems by Robert Fisher, Nash Pollock Publishing, Pages 1-74.
- Poems for Thinking by Robert Fisher, Nash Pollock Publishing, Pages 1-116.
- Natural Knowledge Comprehension Book by Daksha Patel, Olympia Publishers, Pages 68-69.
- A Brief Dictionary of Hinduism by Vedanta Press, Pages 1-87.

The Internet Websites used:

- Wikipedia, the free Encyclopaedia, Swans.
- http://stock.adobe.com, Lions.

TV Shows seen:

- Eastenders, BBC.

NOTES

NOTES

NOTES

NOTES

NOTES

NOTES